For Denise, who
understands our crew!
—A.D.

For Ame.
—S.M.

"Okay…"

BLARP!

ACTION!
MISUNDERSTOOD SHARK
FRIENDS DON'T EAT FRIENDS!
Written by Ame Dyckman
Illustrated by Scott Magoon
SCHOLASTIC INC.

"We all know you
ate me, Shark!"

"IF I ate you...
where's your proof?"

"Hang on.
I don't feel so good."

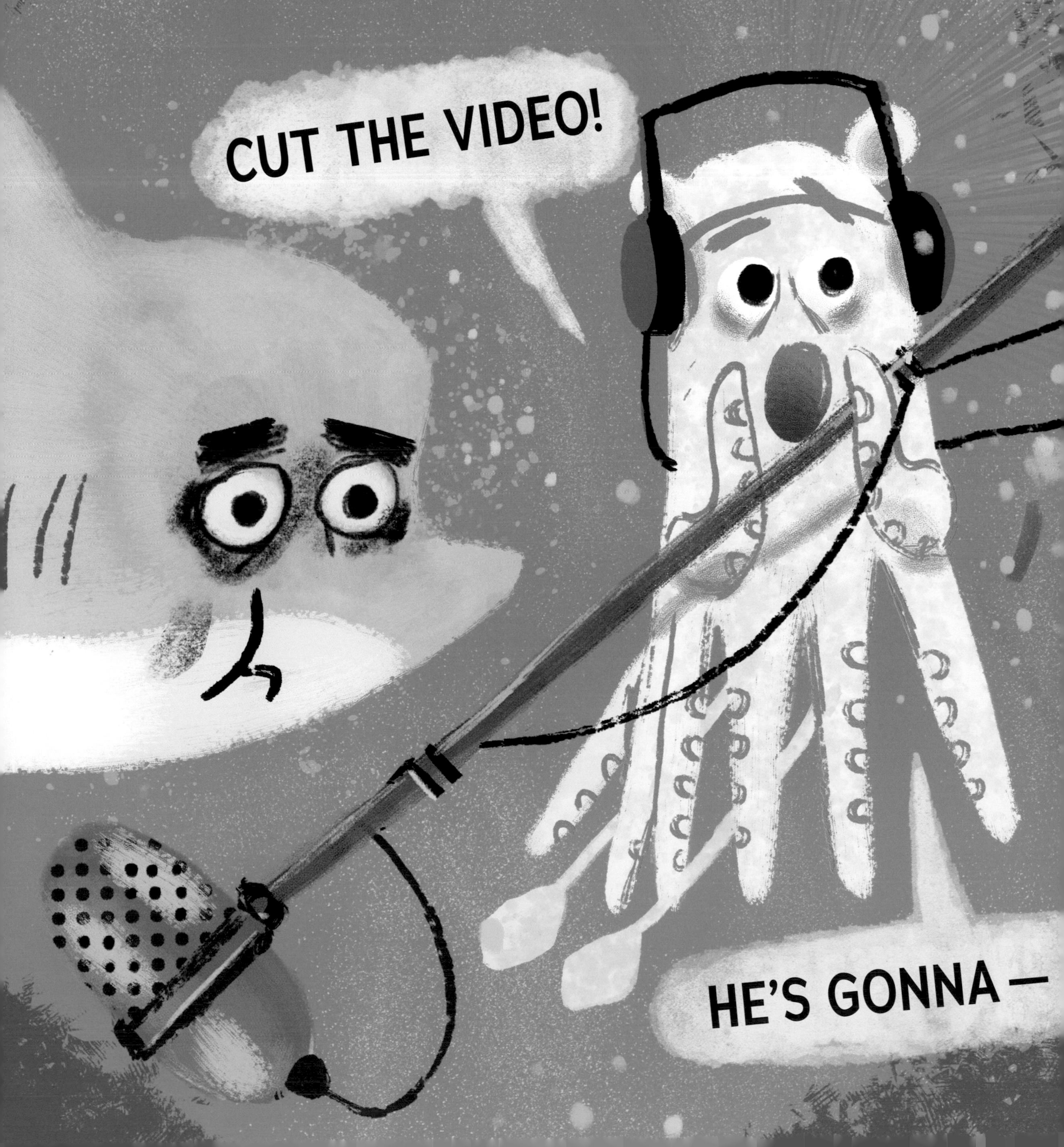

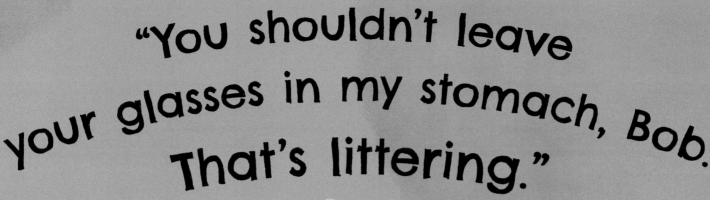

"FRIENDS DON'T EAT FRIENDS!"

"Well . . . FRIENDS DON'T MAKE FRIENDS FEEL BAD ABOUT IT!"

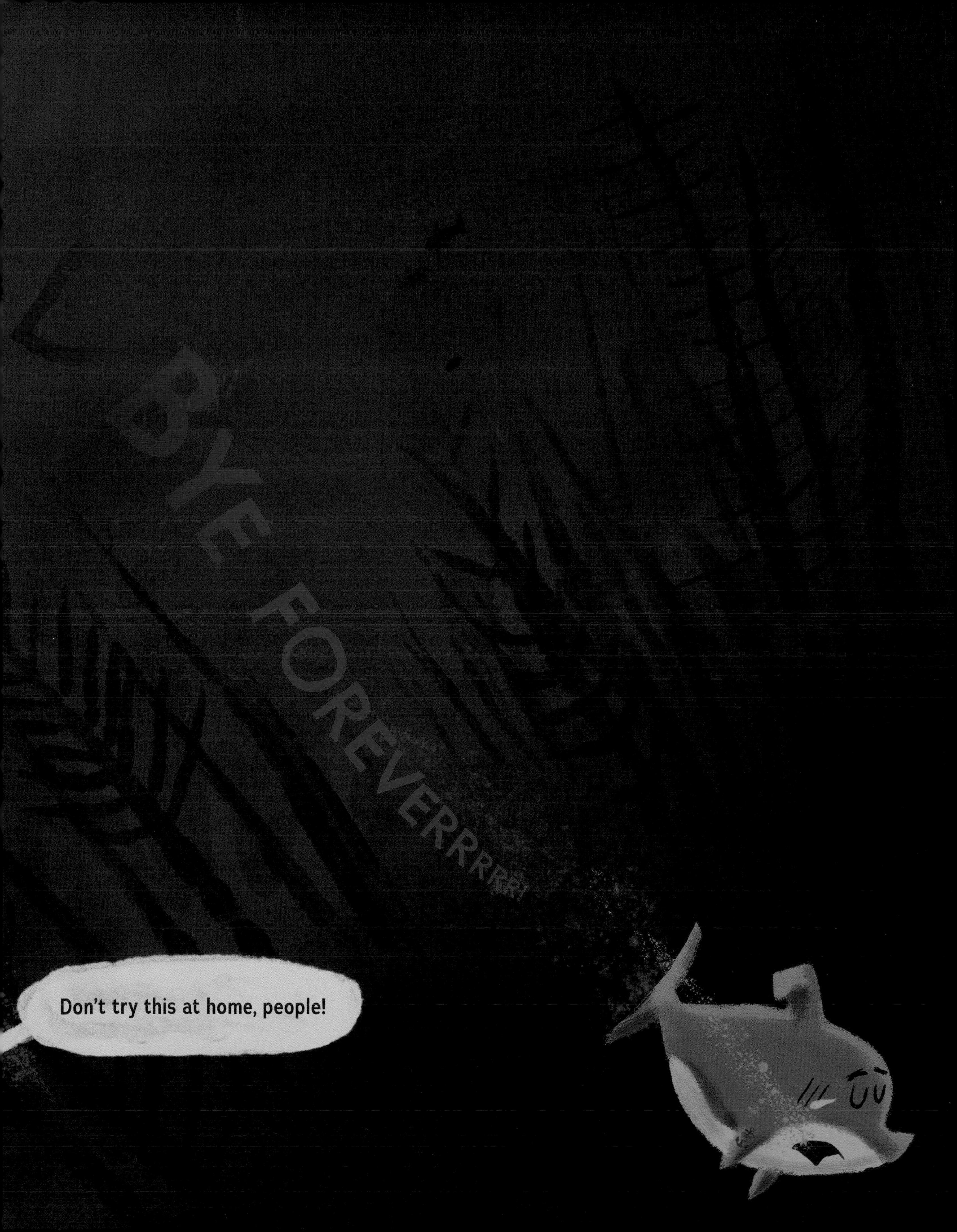
BYE FOREVERRRRR!
Don't try this at home, people!

He's in his Sulking Grotto!
"Go 'way!"
THIS is his feeding frenzy? SUGAR?
You'll get cavities, Shark!

"I do, too!
His name's...
Sticky—"

Is not.

"And he's my
REAL friend—"

Am not.

"And HE'D never hurt
my feelings like
YOU did!"

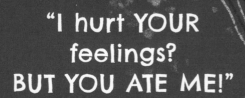

"I hurt YOUR
feelings?
BUT YOU ATE ME!"

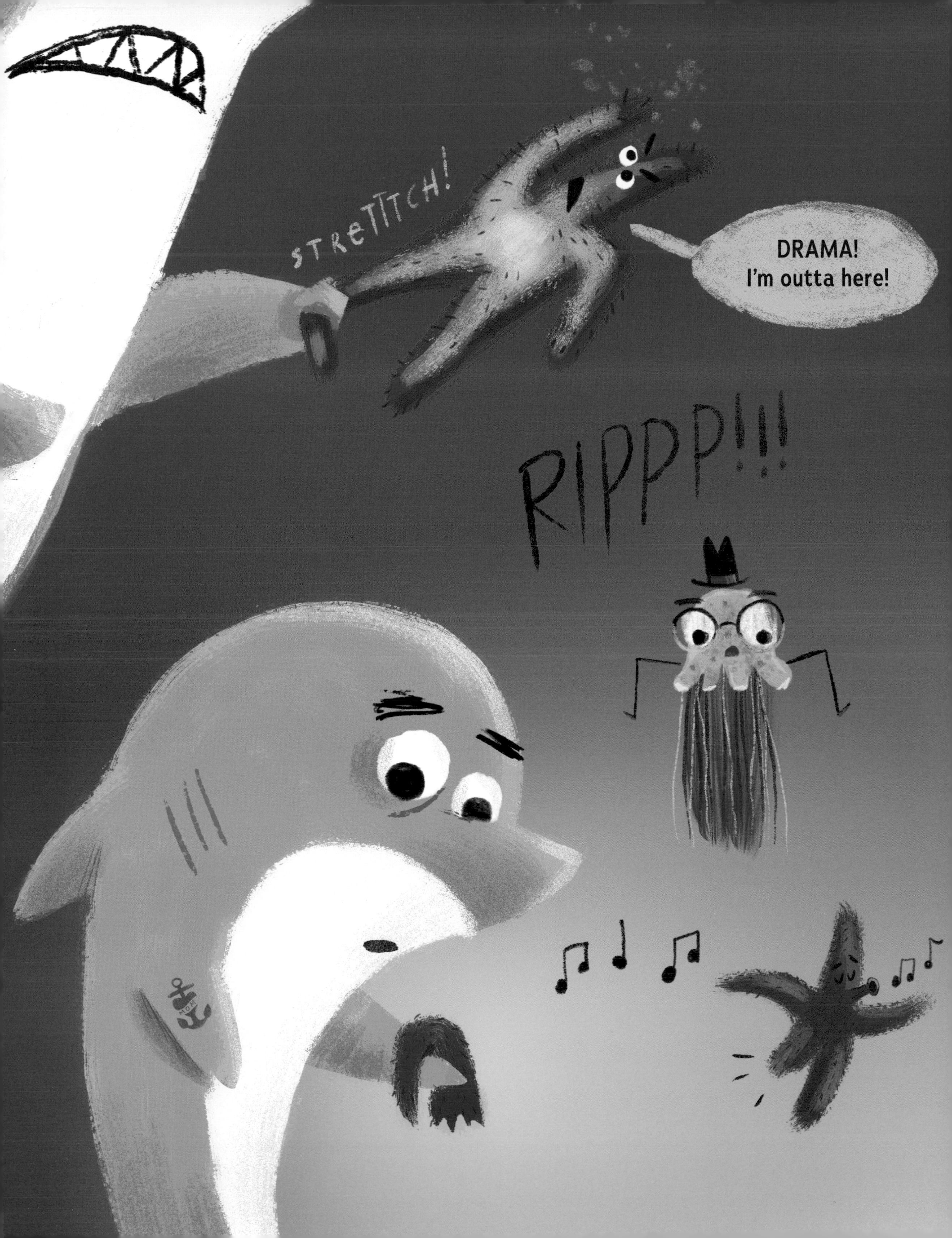
STRETTTCH!
DRAMA!
I'm outta here!
RIPPP!!!
MOM

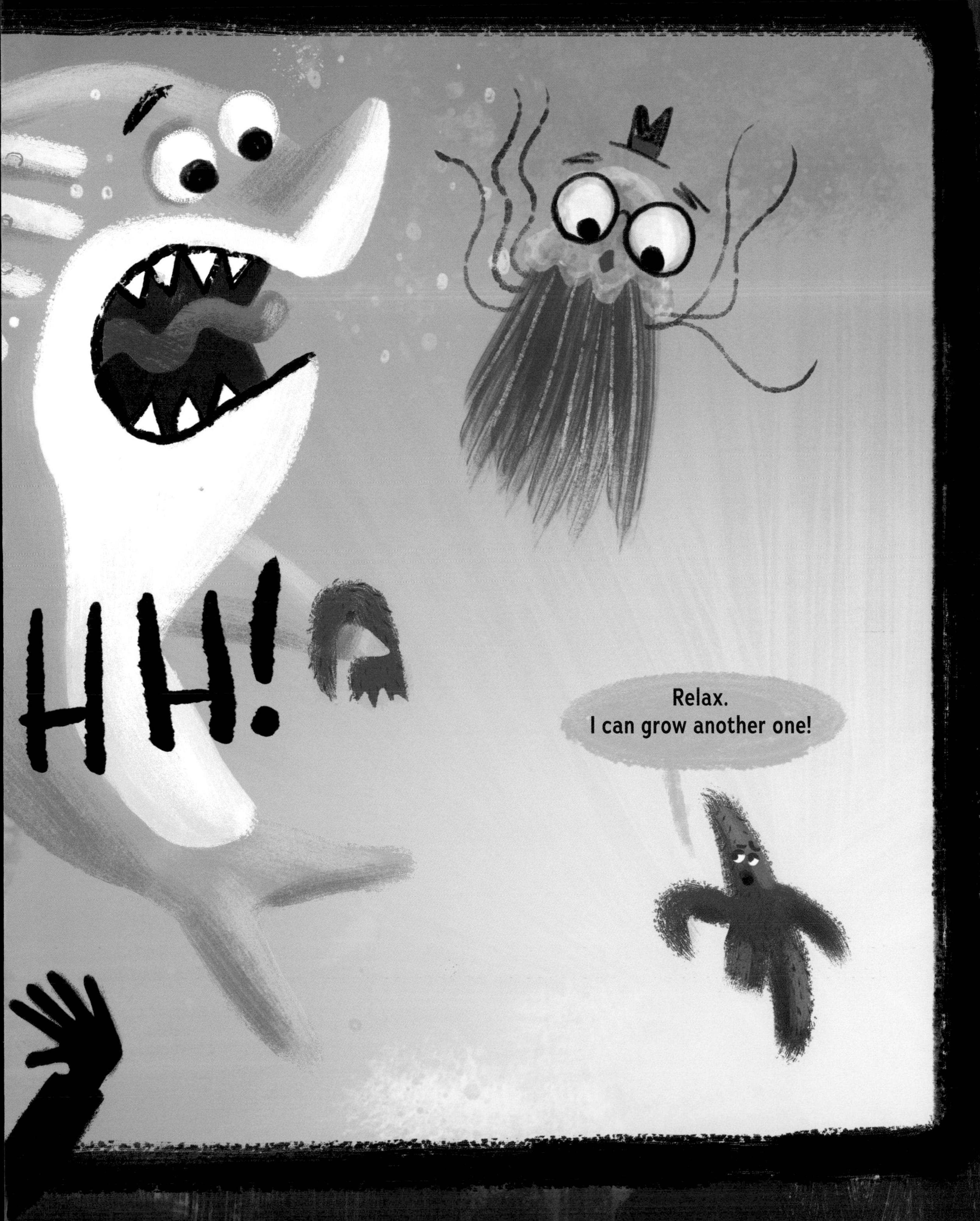
HH!
Relax.
I can grow another one!

"Shark, I'm sorry I hurt your feelings.
I'll try not to hurt your feelings again."

"I . . ."

"Okay, I ate you. I'm sorry and
I'll try not to eat you again 'cause..."

"You taste gross."

"SHARRRK!"

"I mean..."

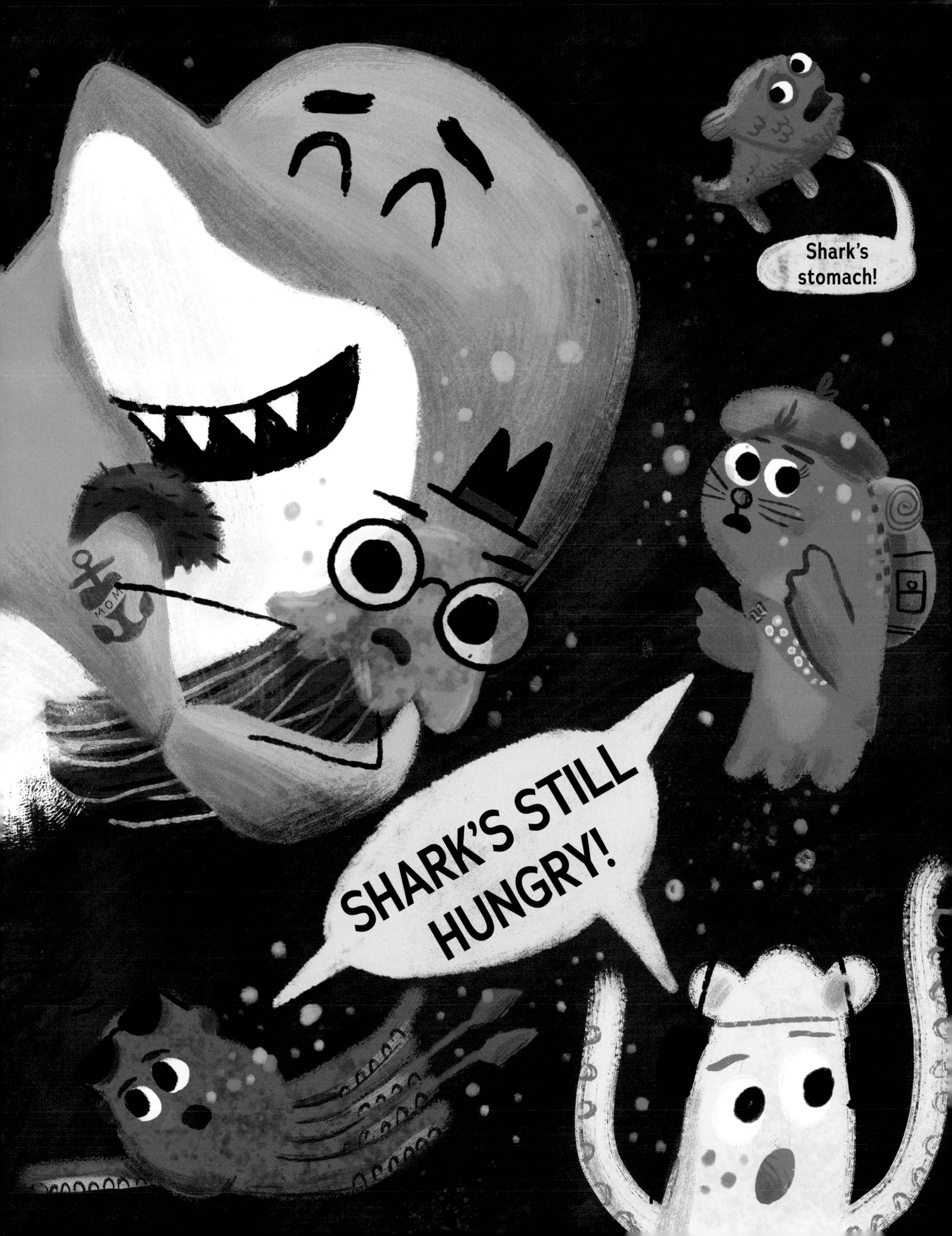
Shark's stomach!
SHARK'S STILL HUNGRY!

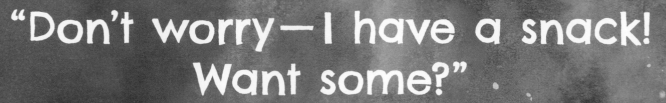

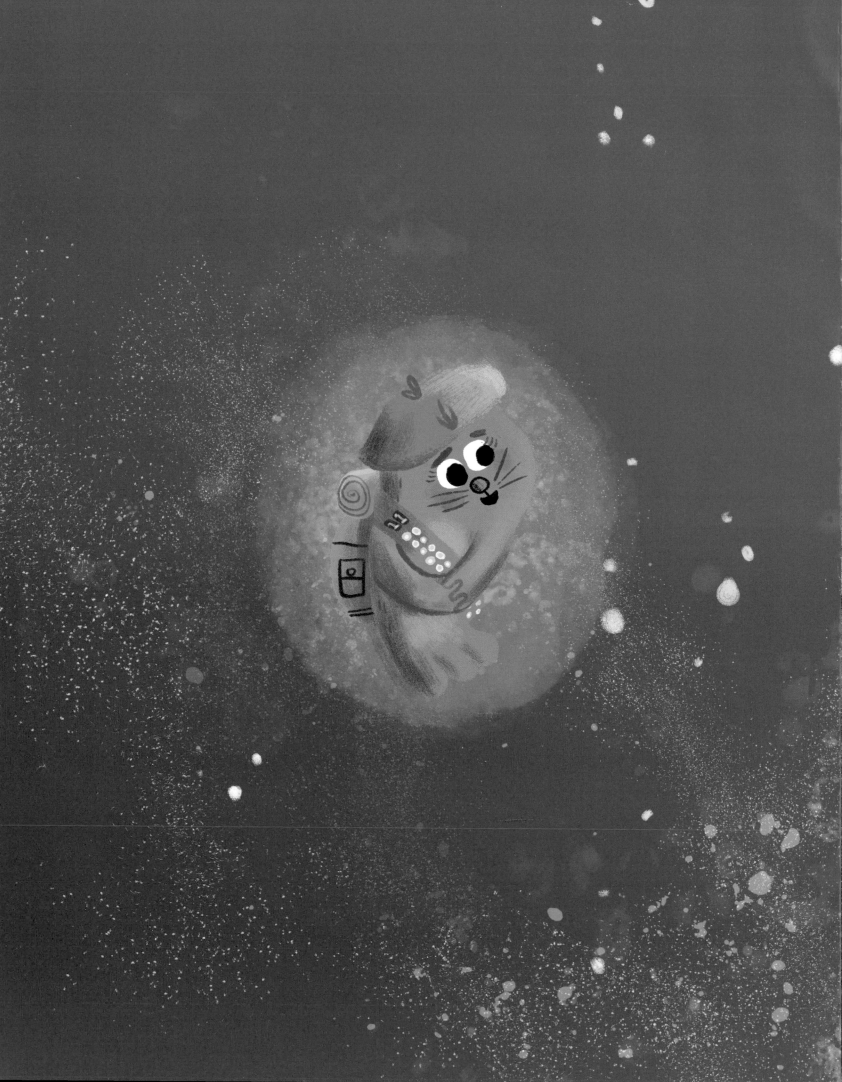